To rule-breakers everywhere—
YOU can change the world. —N.V.

For Kai, Kaden, Sydney, Jonah, and Amalia—
question EVERYTHING. Except for the things I say. —J.L.

Published by Two Lions, New York
www.apub.com

Amazon, the Amazon logo, and Two Lions are trademarks of
Amazon.com, Inc., or its affiliates.

ISBN-13: 9781542043427
ISBN-10: 1542043425

The illustrations were created digitally.
Book design by Andworld Design
Printed in China

First Edition
10 9 8 7 6 5 4 3 2 1

two lions

PRUETT
and SOO

by **NANCY VIAU**

illustrated by **JORGE LACERA**

Planet Monochrome was a teeny tiny planet tucked between Saturn and Jupiter. It blended in nicely with the stars. In fact, no one noticed it at all.

On this planet there lived
a teeny tiny being, Pruett.
As for Pruett?
Well . . .
No one really noticed him either.

Pruett followed the rules at home.

Most of the time.

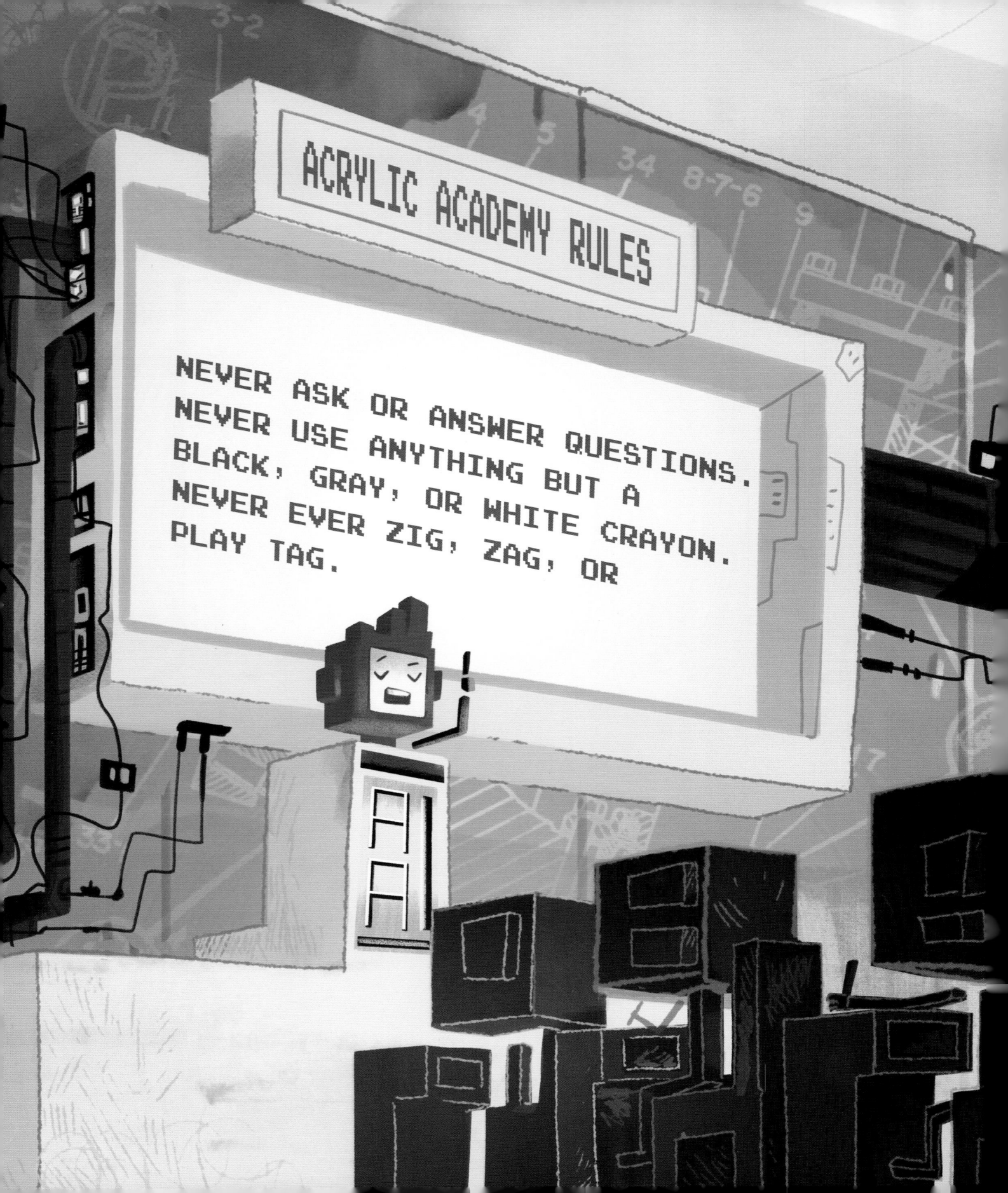

He followed the rules at school.
ALL of the time.
EVERYONE obeyed the school rules.

QUESTIONS!
SOMEONE STOP
HER!

POOPS!! SHE'S
USING COLORS!
TROUBLEMAKER.

NOT
LISTENIIINNNGGG!!
NOT ANSWERING.
I'M PLUGGING MY
EARS.

SIMINY-
ZEEKS!! I'M
MOVIN' TO
EARTH.

"Wowzi!" Pruett said, "She's breaking the rules."

Soo plopped down
next to Pruett.
"What's your name?"

Pruett's ears twitched.
Soo had noticed him!

He wanted to answer her.
But **HE WAS IN SCHOOL!**

The next morning, Soo asked Pruett the same question:
"What's your name? You do have a name, don't you?"

Pruett looked left. He looked right.
He nodded and scribbled "Pruett Levitate" on his worksheet.

Soo didn't stop there. She asked, "Want to color with me?"
Another question! Pruett **did** want to color.
He took out a black crayon and doodled.

"Have you ever zigzagged?" Soo wanted to know.
Pruett loved to zigzag, but he couldn't show Soo.
HE WAS IN SCHOOL!

Soo didn't give up. "Can you zigzag like this?
How about like this?"

Soo zigged up and
down the aisles.
She zagged sideways
across the wall.
She zigzagged out the door
and back in again.

Ms. Z didn't quite know what to do with Soo.

Pruett's cheeks got warm. But he didn't zig a single zag.

Soo called out to Pruett, "Are you sure you don't want to try? Bet those shoes make you superfast."

In the afternoon, Pruett found Soo sitting alone on the playground. She was quiet and still. Her color had begun to fade.

"I wish I could go back to Planet Prismatic,"
Soo said, swiping away a tear.
"Everything here is black, gray, or white.
Blue, turquoise, and violet are much prettier.

And I like asking questions and getting answers."

Suddenly Pruett didn't care about rules.
Even if **HE WAS IN SCHOOL!**

He cared about Sub. And that made him feel brave—
brave enough to ask one question.

"Yes!" Soo shouted. "Finally, someone to play with. You're it!"

"Want to play tag?"

Soo chased Pruett down the sliding board.

Pruett chased Soo across the monkey bars.

When they stopped to grab a drink at the water fountain, Pruett spied his reflection. "Wowzl, look at me! I'm brilliant!"

They colored
here, there, and
everywhere.

They zigzagged to the left
and played tag to the right.

Soon, everyone joined in.

Ms. Z yelled, **"STOP!"** And much to Pruett's surprise, she asked, "What's going on?"

"We're getting to know each other," Soo said.
"What? Why? How? It's against the rules!"

"But," Pruett answered, "if we change the rules, then we can see what makes us special."

Acrylic Academy was never quite the same.

Soo finally felt right at home.

Prueff was happier than he'd ever been.
And **EVERYBODY** noticed.

Well . . .

As for Prueff?